Little Duck Lost

Written by Erica Briers ❄ Illustrated by Stephanie Boey

Dutton Children's Books
New York

On the grassy green riverbank, the bees hummed and the wind whispered lazily.

Then came a rustling and a jostling. A single white egg wobbled down the bank and bumped to a stop in the reeds.

Crack! The shell burst open, and a little duckling wiggled free. He fluffed his feathers and peered at the wide world. He peeped, but no one answered. Little Duck was all alone.

Where am I? wondered Little Duck. He waddled along the riverbank until he spotted a brown frog napping in the sun.

"Are you lost, Little Duck?" croaked the sleepy frog. "The river is not your home. Ducklings belong in the pond."

But before Little Duck could ask him where the pond was, the frog plopped into the river and swam away.

With a wiggle and a waddle, Little Duck continued along the riverbank. Above the gurgle of the water, he heard voices calling to him.

"Quack, quack! Come and swim with us!"

Little Duck wanted to join the wild river ducklings, but the water looked too fast and cold.

"No, thank you!" he peeped. "I've got to find my pond."

With a flop and a hop, he scrambled up the bank. Soon Little Duck came to a shadowy tangle of trees. The bright sunlight of the riverbank seemed very far away.

"Are you lost, Little Duck?" whispered a kind deer.

"Do YOU know where the pond is?" asked Little Duck with a shiver.

"I never leave the forest," explained the deer, "but if you find Rabbit, she will help you."

With a skip and a flap, Little Duck waved good-bye and left the shady forest behind.

Very soon, Little Duck found Rabbit.

"Can YOU help me find my pond?"

Rabbit twitched her nose. "The pond is at the farm. I can't take you there myself, but I know someone who can." Then Rabbit thumped her foot on the ground four times.

Before long, a downy yellow chick came fluttering across the meadow.

"Hello, Little Chick," said Rabbit. "Would you take this lost duckling to the farm?"

"Cheep, cheep!" chirped the fluffy chick. "Come with me!"

Little Duck waved good-bye to Rabbit and ran happily after the chick.

With a shimmy and a shake, they ducked under a fence.

"This is where I live," said the chick. "And here is my daddy!"

The tall rooster gazed sternly down at Little Duck.

"Are you lost, Little Duck? The farm is not your home," crowed the gruff rooster. Then he shooed the little duckling from the farmyard.

With a shiver and a shudder, Little Duck scuttled away.
He felt more lost than ever. Where **did** he belong?

A tear rolled from his eye and dripped from the tip of his bill.

"Don't worry—I can help you!" woofed a loud voice behind Little Duck.

Little Duck nearly jumped out of his feathers when he saw the big farm dog looking down at him.

"Do YOU know where I belong?" he asked.

"Of course," said Dog. "Follow me!"

With a peep and a leap, Little Duck followed the friendly dog straight to the farm pond.

"This is where YOU belong, Little Duck. This is your home," said Dog, giving him a gentle nudge.

"**Yes!** This is where you belong," chorused some ducklings, all fluffy and yellow just like Little Duck.

The water looked calm and warm and inviting. With a dash and a splash, Little Duck plopped joyfully into the pond.

Just then, Mama Duck paddled over, swift and strong. "My lost Little Duck!" she cried. "I've been looking for you everywhere."

"But I found my own way home!" laughed Little Duck.

"So you did," said Mama Duck, and nestled him against her soft white feathers.

With a wiggle and a giggle, Little Duck knew he was exactly where he belonged.